Peter -

TALES OF THE AXE

- All The Best

Go Yanks!

Enjoy -

Ross P. Psuty

ISBN 0-7414-1262-4

Published by:

INFINITY
PUBLISHING.COM

519 West Lancaster Avenue

Haverford, PA 19041-1413
Info@buybooksontheweb.com
www.buybooksontheweb.com
Toll-free (877) BUY BOOK
Local Phone (610) 520-2500
Fax (610) 519-0261

Printed in the United States of America

Printed on Recycled Paper

Published September, 2002

To Nicole Marie,

and in the Memory of

Chris Kammerer,

CONTENTS:

The Darkened Road........................... 1

Sleep Tight, My Angel...................... 14

Woman In White............................... 18

Cyber Axe.. 26

The Old School................................. 37

He Needs Body Parts........................ 47

How To Write A Horror Novel........ 53

I Will Never Let You Go.................. 67

Cabin With A View.......................... 72

Shame On The Night........................ 79

The Neighbor................................... 87

A Warm Place to Stay...................... 95

I am Not A Mad Man...................... 100

The Darkened Road

I wish I had never taken this family trip to Maine. Things might have been different. I might have been different. My family would still be here today, but all because of one night, one night that was supposed to bring our family together. Our small vacation turned into a tragedy. I was told by the doctor to write down this horrible night. I hope by doing so, I will discover a key to why this is happening to me, and my family. I pray this nightmare will come to an end.

My name is Nicholas Banner, and all I can say to my family is, I'm sorry. I never saw anything like this coming, but it seemed like a good idea at the time.

A family vacation, I couldn't see why not. I just wanted to take my beautiful wife Arlene and my 10-year-old stepdaughter Bernadette someplace nice. I didn’t want to take them to some crazy resort or to some boring old country lodge. I wanted them to go out, feel free and see the open land. Get away from our busy life that we know in Baltimore.

It was Bernadette’s idea to go to Maine. I thought she needed this vacation the most. Her mother felt that they were not getting along, and most of the time Bernadette just ignored me until she wanted something.

“Nick,” Bernadette would say, “could you drive me to the mall?”

I hated it when she called me Nick. It was not like that in the beginning. I thought Bernadette used to love me, and I always loved her. I never knew if she accepted me as a father figure or not. Her real father just walked out one day and never returned.

Arlene always reassured me that I was a good father and a great husband. I remembered when I first met my wife. A friend of ours from work set us up on a blind date. We met at a little watering hole inside a Marriott. The hotel was the halfway point of each of our travel distances. She was the most beautiful woman that I had ever seen. Her beautiful long brown hair swayed back and forth when she walked. Her coffee colored eyes shined with love through my soul. That night we sat and talked for hours. Neither of us wanted to go home.

The next three days we saw each other, and on the fourth day, I met Bernadette. It was a magical moment. During the next three weeks, I felt we started to become closer, like a family.

One day Arlene turned to me and asked if she could be my wife. I would have been an idiot not to say yes. We got married four days later, and then I took the three of us on a nice honeymoon trip. I felt that being part of a family should mean being together, and that's just what we did.

I spent as much time that I could with my family. We would go on day trips from time to time. But over the months, work had gotten the best of me, and those trips became less and less frequent. I believe it was my job that put a strain on our family outings. Even Bernadette seemed different. Arlene would tell me that her change was from the hardship of becoming a teenager, but I saw something else, something cold. Maybe it was time for another family trip.

Bernadette asked her mom if we could go to Maine, and when both of them asked me if we could go, I had to say yes. I called my manager at work and told him that I was starting my vacation now. We packed our suitcases and Bernadette mapped out the road directions for our long travel.

The Internet can be a wonderful tool. Just click on the map and find a nice Bed and Breakfast. I told her to map out a nice scenic route for us to take. I did not want to drive the turnpike or a major highway. Driving was half the trip, and I thought exploring the back roads of our country would be a good experience. I knew it would take longer this way, but all we had was time. Time meant not to rush, not to sit at work, not to wake up or go to bed at a set time. Time was free.

We packed the car and started our way to the state of Maine. The drive was more than amazing, it seemed as if our family was reborn and there would be no stopping us from having fun. Along the way we sang songs, joked and waved to the other cars. We had a ball driving through all the different states: New Jersey, New York, Connecticut and New Hampshire. Then we all let out a huge cheer when we finally drove into Maine. What a great time we were having.

The only time that I didn't think about was the time it would take for us to get to Maine. I knew it would be around nightfall, hopefully 7 or 8 p.m. I never thought it would hit midnight.

Sometimes you forget that you're a parent and that there are no such things as taking a road trip all the way through. You forget things such as bathroom breaks, lunch breaks, and "scenic view just ahead" breaks.

I looked at the map that Bernadette had printed out from the computer. I knew that we were in Maine, and I knew that we were near a town called Upton. The map labeled every road sign, bridge and exit ramp around us. But one thing that the map never listed, the one thing that affected my life, was that one road. The long unpaved road filled with blackness from the tall trees and dense woods that surround it.

They never showed this road on the map, but I took it anyway with help from my encouraging family.

"Hey Nick, lets go this way," Bernadette said. "It looks cool."

"I don't think so," I said hoarsely. I hated it when she called me Nick.

"Come on," Arlene responded. "Where's your taste for adventure?"

As I turned onto the darkened road, I could only watch as the skyline above disappeared from my eyes. Not even the light of the moon could penetrate onto this darkened road.

I found out much later that the locals did not use this road, unless you were a doctor of the Hillsborough Wellness Center. Sounds like a pleasant name, if you didn't know it was for the violently disturbed and the criminally insane. I never saw that sign as I continued to drive that dark and bumpy road. Then again, I guess that's not something people would like to advertise.

The road was long. I wondered if I should turn around and head back to the main road. I started becoming annoyed.

"This isn't my idea of a vacation," I muttered

"Relax," Arlene said. "It can't be that much further to the Bed and Breakfast."

"Not much of a shortcut, Bernadette."

"What's the matter, are you scared Nick?" Bernadette asked mockingly. "You're on the right road, relax."

"Hey, we're supposed to be on vacation, remember? Lets all relax," Arlene suggested. She slipped her hand between my thighs.

"Do you mind?" I barked. "I am trying to concentrate on where we are going!"

"Then turn around and find a new road." Arlene shouted back, pulling her hand away.

I looked into all three mirrors, but only darkness could I see. The world seemed to close its door behind me.

"Look up there!" Bernadette said excitedly.

I saw the flashing yellow light that Bernadette had pointed out. At first I thought it was a road construction sign, but as I drove closer, the light turned into two blinking hazard lights from an old white Sedan. The car stood lopsided as a rusted jack held it in place. A tire was laying on the roadside next the car, it looked damage and unusable. As I slowed down to a crawl, my wife asked the same question that I was thinking.

"I wonder where the owner is?"

I did not answer, because I saw someone walking up the road in front of us. I drove up to see a man, I noticed that he was wearing all white, including his pants and jacket. When we were close enough to the man, my beautiful wife Arlene rolled down the window and stuck her head out to see if the man needed any assistance.

I never saw his face, but I saw the shiny object in his hand as he raised it over his shoulder. I wanted to pull Arlene away from the window, but I could not move. All I could do was watch, as this man swung himself around and hit my wife with a large killer instrument.

Her body collapsed on top of mine. She didn't seem to move, as I could feel her warm body lying against my lap. I screamed out her name, but my wife never answered. I looked down to see Arlene's headless body lying there motionless. I screamed again, but this time in horror and then raced my foot onto the accelerator.

I don't remember hitting the tree, but when I awoke from my dizziness, I saw the front end and hood were crushed from the impact. All the doors were wide open as a strong smell of anti-freeze surrounded the car. I looked where my wife was sitting, she was no longer there. I turned around and Bernadette was also missing.

I ran out of the car and checked each side in case they were ejected during the impact. I couldn't find a trace of either one. Maybe it was all a bad dream. Maybe Arlene and Bernadette were okay. Perhaps I had fallen asleep while I was driving and hit the tree. They couldn't wake me up after the accident and went for help.

That's something Arlene would do. She was always so caring. Didn't matter who you were or what you had, she would stop and help out anyone. That was just her nature.

As I walked back to the main road, I knew it had to be a dream, but it seemed so real. I kept asking myself where on the trip did I fall asleep. Before I could finish my train of thought, I saw a shadowy object up ahead.

"It can't be," I remembered saying as I ran to the object that I'd seen before.

The white Sedan sat in its place. "Was it a dream?" I asked myself as I noticed something different. The hazards were no longer on. I wondered if the battery had died. I reached the driver side door, placed my hand through the open window and pulled the switch for the headlights. They lit up the road in front of me. I looked inside the car and saw the keys hanging from the ignition. If I could get this car started, I could go and get help.

After remembering seeing the damaged tire on the road, I knew I needed to change it. I took the keys out of the ignition and walked over to the trunk hoping to find the spare in there. I inserted the key and turned it to the right. The door sprung open, and the light of the trunk flickered on.

Inside, I saw a man in a fishing garment, his body stayed still. His motionless eyes stared back at me. His garment was drenched in blood, as a silver-bladed axe rested across his lifeless body. I was in too much shock to scream when I realized that this was all a true nightmare. So many questions filled my soul, but none had answers.

As I searched for some kind of hope about my missing family, I heard a familiar sound coming towards me. What I saw was a car, as it shined its burning headlights into my worried eyes. The driver stopped.

"Are you okay?" He asked. "I see you have a flat there."

"No, it's not mine," I blurted out. "I need to get to a phone. I need to call the police."

"Well then, you'd better hop on in."

I looked at the man as I climbed into his dark Chevy Blazer. He was wearing black pants and a blue shirt. Feeling a little safer now, I leaned back into the seat. We drove off and continued down the darkened road.

"You might want to take some of these," the man said, and pulled out a small bottle of tablets from his shirt pocket.

"No thanks, I just can't seem to…"

"Trust me, I'm a doctor. Doctor Knofield. The pills will help you calm down, and you'll remember everything that happened tonight when you talk to the police."

I felt better knowing I had a doctor at my side. I took the pills and was about to swallow them whole when the good doctor told me there was some juice in his glove compartment. I opened the compartment in front of me and took the bottle in my hand. My other hand raised the pills into my mouth and I swallowed them down with some very bad-tasting juice.

"Sorry, I guess that's been in there longer than I thought," the doctor said after seeing the bitter look on my face. "We're almost there."

"Where are we going?"

"The Hillsborough Wellness Center is the closest phone you'll find in this area," Doctor Knofield explained. "I should know I work there."

We drove a little further, and I saw my car still hugging tightly to the tree.

"Is that yours?"

"Yes. Are we almost there?" I asked, as I started to feel queasy.

"Only another mile down the road."

"What is the Wellness Center?" I questioned, then something felt heavy in my head.

"It's a clinic for special cases of the mentally disturbed."

"Doc, what's wrong with me?" I slurred. "I feel so dizzy, my head. Everything looks so fuzzy, why can't I..."

When I awoke, I had no idea what happened to me. My head felt heavy with pain. I wished I knew the time and how long I was out for. I noticed I was lying on a white and tan cot and looked around the small room I was in. The walls looked as if they were made of a white sponge on each side of me, except for one wall where the door was. That was all glass. On the side of the bed, on a table, next to the bedpan, was a pad and pencil. On the first page was a written instruction.

"Please write down everything you remember about tonight, signed Dr. E. Knofield."

So that is my story, Dr. Knofield, I hope you and the police can help me find my family.

Nick heard a knock on the glass window. It was the doctor.

"How are you feeling?" Dr. Knofield asked as he spoke through the little voice holes in the glass.

"Better. Now let me out of here so I can find my family," Nick demanded.

"It's almost 5:30 a.m.," the doctor said as he looked down at his silver wristwatch. "Too bad about Mr. Robertson. He usually opens his shop about now."

"What?" Nick Asked. "Wait!" He shook his head, trying to gain some sense of control.

"You see," Dr. Knofield continued, "Mr. Robertson usually goes fishing before he opens his store, but at the time I thought he was you and-"

"Daddy!" A little girl's voice echoed from the hallway.

Nick walked to the glass window. He saw that it was Bernadette as she ran down the hallway towards him. Thank God she's alive, Nick thought.

Bernadette ran to the window. Looked into the glass and started to wave.

"Honey," Nick gleamed. "I'm so happy to see you, I thought I would never see you again."

"Nick?"

"Yes, Angel?" Nick used to hate it when she called him by his first name, but right now he was just so happy to see her.

"I want you to meet my real daddy." She said, hugging Dr. Knofield. "He's a doctor."

"Bernadette?" Nick asked, feeling lost and confused.

"Sorry, Nick," the doctor said. "Like I was saying. I thought Mr. Robertson was you, otherwise I would have never had killed the man. Oh Arlene. Poor Arlene. I'm sorry about what I did to her. She was a good mother. Just too bad we never saw eye to eye. But I knew I couldn't have Bernadette having another father. It just didn't seem right."

Nick could only watch as Bernadette smiled up at her real father.

"You see," the doctor continued. "I would e-mail Bernadette from time to time, and asked her to keep the conversations our little secret. But when she told me about you, and how she wished that I would be her daddy again, I didn't know what to do. So I thought up this Maine trip. I gave Bernadette all the driving directions and points of interest to stop along the way. To my amazement, everything worked out perfectly. Well, except for Mr. Robertson, but right now he and Arlene are in the white Sedan at the bottom of my private lake." Dr. Knofield looked down at his watch again.

"You'll never get away with this." Nick shouted out.

"Well, actually Nick, I already have. I really hope you enjoy your stay here at the Wellness Center. Come on, precious." Dr. Knofield said as he took Bernadette's hand and started to walk down the long white hallway.

"Bye, Nick," Bernadette said happily as she waved good-bye.

Sleep Tight, My Angel

I wish you knew me. It would only be fair because I know so much about you, but if you knew I were here, in your room, I would hate to do what had to be done. Destroying your life would not be easy for me, but you would give me no choice. You can never know that I am here.

If you did sense my presence, I feel that all I have worked for would become meaningless. The time and effort just to get where I am today, into your house, and into your bedroom. I would not want to ruin that. But if you ever looked up to find me, if you ever opened an eye to see me, I would have no choice but to end your existence.

Sleep, my angel, I love the way you look, tucked safely in your nest of blankets. Some might think that you, a grown adult are far too old to be sleeping with a stuffed animal. I don't. I think he's there to protect you. It's nice to feel safe, and maybe one day he will save you. But, until then, I will be here to watch over you.

Five months ago, you came into my life. I saw you at the park playing with your daughter, Stephanie. You looked so innocent as you played on the swings with her. I remember you were wearing your black shorts with the butterfly on the left side pocket.

It's been a long time since you worn those. Last time was when you ran out to buy stain remover for the carpet. I can still see the coffee stain next to the recliner. But, I'll never say a word. Your secret is safe with me.

Please don't wake up. You have no idea how many dollars your life is worth until you are at death's door. Keep still, my angel. Every day I watch you sleep, and every day I repeat my words: Don't wake up. I would hate it if you did. I would hate to use my axe on you too soon.

You probably never noticed me following you home from the park that night. I sat outside on your porch and watched you through the windows. You made pasta for dinner. Then you read "The Adventures of Sammy Sumner," to Stephanie. And that night after you went to bed, I broke into your house and helped myself to your key ring. It was never missing like you thought. I'm sorry I stole it, but it makes it easier for me to come and go as I please.

Sleep, my angel, I am watching over you. I'm always watching you. I know that on Tuesdays, you play tennis with your friend Beth. Thursdays, you go grocery shopping to beat the weekend crowd, and every morning of the week, you're off to take Stephanie to school, and you're there again every afternoon to pick her up. Every afternoon except Fridays, you let your ex-husband play his daddy part.

Maybe if I pulled the covers off just a bit, I could get a tease. I wouldn't do that. I would not hurt you.

Sleep now, angel, I'm here for you. I'll protect you from all evil. It's Friday and you and I are alone in this big house. Your daughter will be away for the next three days. But I'll be here. Unlike your husband who walked out, I would never do that to you.

I can't see why he left. Maybe he doesn't see your beauty the way I do. I remember the day he came to visit, you argued about child support. His response came with his hand across your face. I wanted to kill him after I saw him slap you. I would have risked it all to save you. But I held back and waited, waited for him to leave. I followed him home, and took away something that he loved very much.

Remember April? I'm sorry he lied to you. She was never just a friend. They had been dating before you signed for the divorce. I was so full of anger when she told me this, that I tied her to a tree and left her. In the back of my mind I still can hear her screaming in sorrow. You don't have to worry about her, the forest is too deep and secluded for anyone to find her. April is gone, she had no one to protect her, not the protection in which you have from me.

You can sleep in peace, angel. I have the whole house under my protection, and by doing so I needed to drill some holes into the attic floor. I hope you don't mind, but I needed to watch you more carefully. I have one hole looking down into the kitchen, one to the bedroom, two in the living room, and one for the Jacuzzi in the bathroom. Just think of them as your own private security system.

It's almost four in the morning. I have to go hide soon, my angel. I hope you will remember that I will always be here to keep an eye on you. Whether you go in the kitchen, the cellar, or the garage, I will always be here for you. Sleep tight, my angel.

Woman In White

"Did I ever tell you the time when I met this woman?" The Grandfather asked his two grandsons. They looked up at him as they sat on the floor with their Tonka trucks. They watched him rock back and forth in his favorite rocking chair. He continued his story before they even had a chance to answer.

"You see, I just turned 16, and a friend of mine, Paul Masters surprised me with a little birthday party. We met in the middle of town one day and he said to me, 'Roy, my dad and I are putting in a well behind our house and we just wanted to know if we can borrow your father's pitchfork.'

"I knew that the back of Paul's house was very wooded, so I knew my father wouldn't mind. Plus, I have never seen Paul work a day in his life. This should be fun to watch.

"Paul gave me a time of ten o'clock that night to drop off the pitchfork. I thought this was strange at first, unless they were going to start early the next morning and wanted to make sure that they had all the equipment.

"It took me a good 45 minutes to walk from my house to his. When I got to the front of his house, I knocked hard against the solid oak door. No answer. I tried again, and to my surprise, a man that I have never seen before answered. This man was big. He was so big that I didn't think he was a man. I think he was really a bear in man's clothing."

The grandfather looked down at the two young boys to see if they understood the comparison. By their blank expressions, they didn't seem to.

"Anyway, the huge man didn't talk much. So I spoke up first and asked if he knew where Paul was. The man looked down at the pitchfork that I held in my hand, then back at me.

"He asked me if my name was Roy. When I answered yes, he told me that Paul indeed was expecting me, but not here. He wanted me to meet him at the big white cabin.

"Although I heard of this cabin, I had never been there. What I did know is that it was deep in the woods, past the old cemetery. I heard many stories about that cabin, the kind that would keep you up all night.

"I didn't tell the huge man that I heard those stories. I didn't want him to think I was scared. But I did ask him how I should get there. The huge man cleared his throat and started to give me directions.

'Follow the dirt path that leads into the woods.' The man said. 'That path will take you to the cemetery. Keep walking until you come to a crooked cross. The cross leans to the right. That's the direction that you want to go in. Keep walking until you come to a clearing. Now, in the middle of that clearing, you'll see the big white cabin. Can't miss it.'

"Before I could be on my way, the huge man stopped me with his words. 'You don't need that,' he said as he pointed to my father's pitchfork. 'Leave that here, it's for your own safety.'

"So I left the pitchfork with the man and headed into the woods. During my journey, I started to think about the stories I had heard. People used to say that the white cabin was built back in the early 1800s. They said a man built the place for himself and his daughter, while others say that it wasn't his daughter, but his mistress. The daughter just happened to catch the two of them together, and he dragged her into the cemetery and buried her alive."

The grandfather noticed that the children were starting to pay more attention to him. He cleared his throat, reached over to the table next to him.

Picked up his favorite pipe, clutched it between his teeth and lit the tobacco. The smooth vanilla aroma escaped his mouth and hovered around the room.

"I didn't know what stories to believe. But I did know that the cabin existed and I believed Paul was there, waiting for me. I walked about two miles before reaching the cemetery. I had only seen this place in the daytime, and even then it looked scary to me.

"The headstones were old and giving away. The tall grass and trees densely covered the entrance as if to keep visitors like me out. The wind pushed me closer to the cemetery, but before I entered I took control of my fears and told myself not to be afraid.

"When I stepped into the realm of the rested, I told myself to look straight at all times. Not to let shadows or noises distract me. Slowly I walked, as the light of the moon guided me through the maze of tombstones. All I could hear was the wind rustling through the trees, and the long dried grass, as it brushed across my legs.

"Before long, I saw the crooked cross in my view. I turned right and made my way through the overgrown bushes until I came to a clearing. In front of me stood the white cabin. I heard voices and laughter coming from the inside.

"I opened the door to see Paul and the rest of my friends. They were dancing and having a delightful time."

'Roy,' Paul shouted. 'You have arrived.'

"Everyone cheered and wished me a happy birthday. I realized that this was all for me. My friends lifted me in their arms and carried me around the room for all to see.

"I danced with some lovely maidens and joked with my fellow neighbors. I even had a pie-eating contest with my best friend Paul. He won.

"We partied late into the night. I had a feeling it was past my curfew, and needed to get home. I said good-bye to Paul and my friends, and left the big white cabin.

"When I started to walk back home, I gave myself the same rule as before. Look straight at all times. Not to let shadows or noises distract me. But, like in life, there are too many distractions before you can reach your goal.

"For me it was the noise of a soft cry. A woman's cry of sorrow is what I heard, and I decided to find out what was wrong.

"I stepped off the trail and went deeper into the cemetery. I came upon a small clearing, and there in the middle stood a white marble bench. She was sitting there with her head buried in her hands, weeping. As I walked closer, I noticed she was wearing a long white gown. It looked like it was once beautiful, but now it was torn and coated with mud. I was just about to ask her what was wrong when she looked up at me."

'Don't touch me!' She shouted in a deep southern accent.

"I jumped back, then tried to calm her down. I felt it would take some time for her to trust me, she seemed very nervous. I promised her that I would not touch her. I just wanted to know why she was crying.

"She started telling me about a man who would always be drunk and then slap her or touch her, depending on the mood he was in. She said it would drive her crazy.

"It drove me crazy just listening to her story. The part that hurt me the most was that she didn't look any older than 14-years of age.

"The wind blown across our faces as she told me that she wanted to poison him, but never found the courage to go through with it. I told her I would have. Her blue tearing eyes looked into mine."

'You would murder your own father?' she asked.

"I felt faint at that moment, and sat down next to her. She jumped up quickly and warned me again not to touch her. I wanted to apologize, but found myself speechless. She sat back down and continued her story."

'Yes, it was my father,' she said. 'My mother died when I was only seven. My father was never the same after that. We moved deep into the woods, and he built us a home. But he was never there. He was always at the pub drinking himself crazy.'

'I broke into his work room.' She started to cry at the same time. 'I took his axe. I told myself if he touched me one more time, I would have no choice but to use it. I hid behind his favorite rocking chair, and waited for him to come home. I'd almost fallen asleep when he finally returned. My body felt numb, and the axe started to feel heavier in my hands. He was looking for me as I heard him call out my name. By the tone of his voice I knew why he wanted me.'

'Kassia,' he would say. 'Where's my beautiful girl?'

'That's the only time he would call me beautiful. I hated him for that.'

"She wiped her tears away, then looked up into the darkened sky and continued her words of sadness."

'I wish it didn't happen. I thought I could hold it, but the axe slipped out of my hand and hit the floor. He came over to me. I had to think quickly, I picked up the axe and jumped out from behind his chair. My legs became weak from sitting on the floor too long. I stumbled and fell. He tried to catch me. I know he did. The axe hit the floor first and then I landed on top. The blade of the axe went through my rib-cage.'

"She opened up her white gown and showed me the long scar which laid across her chest and heart. A cold chill ran down the back of my neck. I felt so bad for her that I did the one thing that she asked me not to do. I touched her. It was on her shoulder. She turned to me and gave me a disappointed look.

“She stood up and walked away from me. I hurried up after her, but she vanished into the mist. I felt numb and asked myself if this just happened.

“I walked back to the path and found myself in front of the crooked cross. The moonlight above shined onto the engraved letters that spelled out these words.

‘Here lies my beautiful daughter, Kassia Rose Lemel. Always will be missed, but never forgotten.’”

Cyber Axe

"It was just about dawn when I saw her eyes turn into a golden look of sunshine, and without her sunshine, I could never have grown into the man that I see in me today. A man who was once trapped in a dark shell of depression, saved by a woman who he will never see again."

"Roger, that was beautiful." Joan wrote back on her keyboard. She sat there in the small back room of the house she shared with her husband. It was almost three in the morning as she typed away softly so not to wake him.

"You let a part of me reveal something that I don't often share with others," the words shined back onto Joan's computer screen.

"Why aren't you an author? I think romance readers would buy your books in a second. I know I would be the first in line," she sent back.

"Joan, you're too kind. But really, it's just a hobby of mine."

"But just think how much money you can make from suckers like myself."

"Money is not important to me. Plus, I do very well."

"I know." Joan kept on pushing Roger to write a book. She thought that he was very talented. "But you should really let yourself shine instead of being so secretive."

"I'm not really. I just have a hard time expressing myself," Roger responded.

"I don't know why. You don't have to hide your feelings around me. It is not like we'll ever meet."

"Joan, are you writing what I think you're writing?"

"It doesn't matter. I'm married, anyway."

"Don't do this to yourself, thinking about us and what could have been."

"I know it's only been a few months, Roger, but you're so different. Different than any other man I've chatted with. Every time I've gone to a chat room it is, 'Hey baby, want to do a little cyber sex?' Like that really works. But you're not like that at all. Maybe you should write a book on how to be a real man."

"I might agree with you there, but I don't think most men would buy it. Not many of us like to change."

"I think it's funny that you live in the next state from me." Joan Typed.

"187 miles."

"You know the mileage?"

"I was playing around with the computer maps, and from your town to my house in big Hallsville, Texas is only 187 miles."

"Oh my God, that's even closer than I thought. I could probably drive there before night fall."

"Joan, don't get any crazy ideas."

"By the way, I love how your hair has that little curl in front."

"Excuse me?" Roger responded.

"I'm looking at the picture you sent me a while back. Are you still this handsome?" Joan asked

"I thought you said you deleted that picture."

"I lied."

"Joan, I thought you never lied."

"I have to go. I think I hear my husband."

As Joan's name faded off Roger's instant message screen. He heard a voice behind him.

"What are you doing?" Roger's girlfriend asked.

"Kelly, you startled me." Roger said sitting in his oversized leather chair as he turned off his computer. "I just had to finish up a few things before sunshine comes in."

"Your stupid little phases are getting old," Kelly said.

Before she could leave the room, Roger grabbed her by the arm and pulled her onto his lap. "You used to like it way back when."

"Oh, yeah," she said with sarcasm in her voice. "Three months ago, wow!"

"I don't want to argue. Besides, I have something for you. Been saving it for a while."

"What is it?" Kelly asked cheerfully.

"Come with me and you'll find out."

Kelly got up and started following him down the hallway.

"Where are we going?" She questioned.

"It's down in the cellar." Roger answered.

"No, I hate it down there." Kelly stopped. "It's so creepy. I feel like someone is watching me. Why don't you bring the present up here?"

"Come on, you'll love it," Roger smoothly coaxed her.

"Really?"

"Really. Please take my hand."

Joan woke up late that morning and walked down to the kitchen as she pulled on her bathrobe. Her husband Tim was there eating a bowl of cereal.

"You woke up late again I see," he said in a hard tone.

"Sorry, Tim. Don't know what's wrong with me."

"Third day in a row." Tim looked down into his bowl. "This cereal won't get me very far today."

"Sorry, did you want me to make you some eggs?" She asked.

"No, I'm already late." Tim got up from the kitchen table and threw the bowl into the sink. "I think we should have a little talk when I get home from work." He continued without looking at her, grabbed his hardhat and left for work.

Joan sat down where he was sitting and started to cry. She hated Tim's lectures on how to be the perfect housewife. "Oh Roger, I wish you were here," she whispered.

She ran into her small computer room and turned it on. She sat there impatiently as it warmed up. When the computer screen came on, Joan went to the instant message board and started to write to Roger.

Even though Roger was not online, she was sure he would get the message when he logs on.

"I'm writing this to you now, because my life is hurting here. I'm exhausted from my husband abusing me. I feel that I need to run far, far away. This might be the last time you'll hear from me. I wish things could be different. I do. But as I sit here writing you this letter, I can only think of how my life is meaningless in my husband's eyes. I need something more, someone more. I need someone like you in my life. I don't know where I'm going, but I have to go."

She hit return and wiped the tears from her eyes. When she looked back up at the screen, something new had flashed in.

"I don't think your life is meaningless." The instant message popped up.

"Oh Roger, don't do this to me. I just need to go. Please don't make this harder for me."

"Where are you going to stay?"

"I don't know, but I need to leave and now." Joan quickly typed back.

"Then come and stay with me."

"You make it sound so easy."

"It is," Roger responded. "I'm only in the next state. I'll write down the directions and keep the porch light on for you."

"You hardly know me."

"I hate to see you out there on your own. Plus there are too many crazy people out there. Please. Stay with me."

It took Joan only a half-hour to pack some of her things, fill the Jetta with gas and get on the highway to see Roger. She could not believe she was doing this. She felt strange, yet excited at the same time. She felt pangs of guilt for leaving her husband.

In less then four hours she had reached Roger's home. The directions he had giving her were very simple. His blue colored house was large with black shutters surrounding each window. As Joan walked up the stone filled driveway, she noticed that not many neighbors were to close to his home.

She reached for the doorbell, but found a note taped around it. “It’s open.”

Joan was unsure if the message was for her, but she walked in. The entrance looked like a museum. Abstract paintings hung from the walls, as half-naked statues were placed on top of ivory pedestals.

The next room Joan entered was the kitchen. She walked across the black marble tile and saw another note taped to one of the white wooden panels.

“Joan, please make yourself at home. I’m sorry I was not here to greet you in person, but business calls. I will see you soon, my sunshine.”

A tour of the house seemed the best way to kill some time as she waited for Roger to come home. Joan decided to check out the upstairs first. She walked up the long spiral staircase and opened the first door. It was the bathroom with a Jacuzzi tub. Joan peeked into the next four rooms, they were all bedrooms, and each one designed in a unique style. The fifth room was the computer room. She smiled to herself, as she thought that this is where it all started, on the Internet.

Downstairs, Joan found a long oak table and a dozen chairs in the dinning room. The next room was filled with bookshelves installed into the walls. In the center of the room was a medieval-looking chair, and next to that was a chess set with Egyptian pieces resting on a small iron table.

The TV room housed a projection screen and five rows of couches in a theatre-like setting. Next to that was a sitting room with leather sofas and chairs.

At the end of the downstairs hallway was a door that was painted black. Joan opened the door and saw stairs leading down into darkness. She flicked a switch on a wall. Nothing happened. Joan walked down the steps, and when she reached the bottom, she felt a string hovering above her. She tugged on it, and a yellow bulb lit up her surroundings. Joan got startled when she saw the armored knights standing on each side of her. But realized that they were only decorations.

Behind the knights, a wall of stone held different varieties of medieval battle-axes. Above the axes were heads of large gargoyle statues. But the last gargoyle's head didn't have an axe. To her left was another door, a red light shined from underneath. Joan placed her hand on the doorknob.

"That room is not yet finished," she heard a voice say. Joan turned around and was startled to see Roger standing before her. "Sorry," Roger continued. "I didn't mean to scare you."

"Oh Roger, I'm happy to see you." She jumped into his arms and kissed him. "I feel so relieved, so fresh, and so real right now. I need to thank you for that."

"Well, before you do, I hope that you're hungry. I make a great swordfish."

Roger took her hand and led her back upstairs and into the kitchen.

They ate dinner and talked about everything. "Whoever thought this would happen?" Joan asked. "I mean here I was this boring housewife, and now I'm here in this beautiful house." She stopped and looked around the large dining room again. "You have such a beautiful house."

"Thank you. I hope you had no problem finding the place?" Roger asked.

"No, the directions were easy." She took a deep breath out of her fantasy and asked him a serious question. "Do you mind if I ask you what you do for a living?"

"Appraisals," he said. "I work for different museums. Before they purchase these great works of art, they pay me to look at it. I tell them what year a certain piece was made and how much the piece would be worth. It's a good living."

"I'm very impressed." Joan said as she rubbed her tired eyes.

"You're welcome to use one of the guest rooms."

"Yes, that would be fine."

Roger showed her to the upstairs bedroom. The walls were a soft pink, and the carpet looked to be a mix of a darker shade of pink. There were two dressers in the room and they both had a vase filled with roses in them. The queen size bed stood in the middle of the room. The plum-colored sheets were silk, the oversized pillows a light sky blue.

"This will be perfect," Joan said.

"Where is your suitcase?" he asked.

"You know, I never took it out of the car."

"Would you like me to get it for you?"

"No, I can get it in the morning. I can't think of anything that I really need right now."

Roger left the room as Joan slipped into the bed. Her dreams about running away had come true, but she was not sure on how to handle it. Her thoughts were rumbling in her head as she fell asleep.

Joan awoke, as she felt the weight of someone on her bed. Roger started to kiss her neck, then her lips. She was now sure that running away was the best thing she did. That night she let Roger have all of her. She felt connected to paradise.

Later that night, Joan awoke hearing a noise. "Roger!" she shouted, and climbed out of bed and went down the hallway. She looked into the other rooms, and opened the door to the computer room. Roger was not there, but the computer was on. Joan went over to the computer desk.

"Roger are you still there?" The words shined from the screen. "I hope that we are still on for Sunday night. Love your sunshine, Lacy."

Joan ran downstairs, looking for Roger. She passed the dining room, the kitchen, the TV room, and the sitting room. Joan heard the noise again, but they were not coming from any of those rooms. It was coming from the cellar.

She opened the cellar door. The yellow light was shining brightly. Joan followed the noise down the stairs and to a door at the end of the room. Joan could hear a voice yelling the name Kelly from the other side of the door.

Her hand reached out to the doorknob. Slowly, she started to twist it. Suddenly, the doorknob flew out of her hand and swung inward. There she saw Roger standing in a white surgical gown, which was full of blood. He stood there motionless, and holding a large battle-axe in his hand. Joan gasped when she saw pieces of a woman's body behind him. Arms and legs were scattered across the blood-covered floor. Roger grabbed Joan as she let out a horrified scream.

"I like to make sure my ex's are always mine," Roger explained. "And you're next."

The Old School

"In the small town of New Brunswick, New Jersey, behind all the glamour shops and flashing stop lights, there lies an abandoned school, but it wasn't always abandoned. There was a time before the overgrown weeds and vines covered its surroundings. Where there were students and teachers roaming those empty halls.

But that all changed when the police found human bones in a hidden room behind the janitor's closest. The townspeople blamed the janitor. They said he was the one who did it, that he was an odd individual.

Before police could question him, he disappeared. No one knows what happened to him.

Some say that he still roams the school waiting for his next victim."

"Yeah okay, Brad." Michael said. "I might be new in your town, but that doesn't mean you can tell me ghost stories all day."

"No, it's true." Brad answered back. "Just ask anyone in town. They'll tell you."

"I don't believe you," Michael said, as he walked away.

It was a difficult time for Michael, moving into a new town, going to a new school, and even making new friends. He had been living in town for only 2 weeks, and he had never heard about any story about the old school. Why should he believe Brad anyway? Michael knew better than believe about some crazy old janitor, who roams the halls looking to slaughter people.

On his way home, Michael decided not to take his usual route. He decided to walk a different way, a route that took him pass the old school. Michael felt he knew what he was doing. That's what he told himself many times as he walked down the sidewalk. Michael wanted to know if there was any truth to these rumors.

Michael walked three miles before he reached the other part of town. For some reason it didn't look as nice. He noticed more litter, which cluttered the streets. Traffic seemed to be less visible along these roads. The buildings around him looked mostly deserted and falling apart.

At the end of the block he noticed a large field had opened up in front of him. The yellow wheat grass was long and dead, and an old rusted fence surrounded the property. He looked out past the tall grass and saw the old school standing alone. The site memorized Michael as he noticed most of the windows were boarded up, and where there once were opened doors, now were locks and chains.

It would be getting dark soon, and he knew he had to be back home. His parents would worry. Even though Michael was fifteen and he felt he knew how to take care of himself. He didn't like to worry his parents, especially being in a new town and not knowing many people.

The next afternoon, Michael saw Brad at school.

"Hey, Mike," Brad started. "Sorry if I scared you yesterday."

"No, you didn't scare me," Michael answered back. "I knew those stories weren't true."

"No, they're true all right," Brad, stated.

"Listen, I saw the school. It was locked up tight. No one can get in or out of there."

"Billy Martin did," Brad explained.

"Who?"

"Billy Martin. He found a way in one night."

"Yeah, okay, Brad."

"No, trust me." Brad said. "I was there. He went in and never came out. Actually, he was a lot like you."

"What do you mean, like me?" Michael asked harshly.

"Billy didn't believe in the rumors either. So he and a few of our friends went to the school one night. We stood in front of it, and dared each other to go in. Billy took the dare. He was certain that nothing was going to happen to him. He went in and never came out."

"Maybe he went home, maybe he was playing a joke on you for waiting," Michael said.

"That's what we thought at first, until…"

"Until what?"

"Until we heard a scream," Brad continued. "We think it was Billy, but we didn't bother standing around to find out. We ran back home, and still to this day, nobody knows what happened to him."

"Brad, I told you these scary stories wouldn't work on this new kid."

"Okay, tough guy, why don't you meet me and a few of my friends up there tonight, at midnight. Then we'll see how brave you are."

"Fine, I'll be there," Michael, said proudly.

The boys went their separate ways. Michael walked out onto the school's parking lot. He never heard the car drive up to him.

"Hey Mike," a female's voice yelled out.

The voice startled Michael at first. "Hey! Nice car Joy."

Joy was the first person Michael had met in his class. He watched her park her red Trams-Am next to him and stood up out of her T-top. She wasn't born in the 60's, but tried to dress the part. Her dark blonde hair was in long braids. Michael then noticed her clothing. She was wearing a pair of bell-bottom jeans and a brown denim jacket with fringe.

"Where are you hanging?" She asked.

"Nowhere, I'm on my way home."

"Sounds, cool," Joy sat back into the car seat. "Hey, I saw you talking to that weirdo Brad kid."

"He's okay," Michael said unconvincingly.

"Yeah, but be careful. He and his loser friends like to tease the life out of people."

"Don't worry, I can take care of myself." Michael ensured her.

"Okay, I hope to see you tomorrow." Joy placed her car in drive and raced away.

"I hope so." Michael whispered to himself, he wasn't sure if he should go through with this dare tonight. Michael also felt that if he didn't do the dare, Brad would continue to tease him.

That night, before midnight, Michael dozed into a deep dream. He pictured himself running down a darkened hallway at the old school. Close behind him was an old man, who had scars upon his face. The man limped awkwardly with each step he took. In his right hand he carried an old rusty meat hook. The bloodstains that covered the hook chipped away as it was being dragged across the hallway lockers.

The faster Michael would run, the closer the old man seemed to get. Michael could hear the screeching noise of the hook, as it seemed to be getting closer. In front of him was a pair of doors that lead outside. He could sense the old man's breath on the back of his neck.

The doors were now at his reach. With all his might, Michael pushed at the doors, but the powerful chains held them closed. With all hope taken away from him, Michael knew that he had lost. He laid his head against the locked door and waited for death to come.

A loud buzzing noise of his alarm clock woke Michael from his bed. It was 10 to midnight. He ignored his dream and went out to meet Brad at the old school.

Brad and his friends were already waiting when Michael arrived.

"Didn't think you were going to show," Brad remarked as he leaned against the school's rusted fence.

"Yeah, we thought maybe you were too chicken to go in." One of Brad's friends spoke out.

"No, I'm here like I promised," Michael replied, as he sounded up for the challenge.

"Well you may be here, but you're not in there," Brad said pointing to the old school in front of them. "And that's what we came here to see."

Michael looked at the school, and then took a deep breath. "I'm going in."

Brad seemed surprised, but tried not to show it. Michael walked through the opening of the fence, and treaded through the long wild grass. Before long, he had reached the school. Most of the bricks looked cracked and discolored. Graffiti scattered the walls, as broken beer bottles covered the edges around the school.

After circling the area, he saw a piece of wood hanging off one of the broken windows. It was a way in. Michael pushed the wood aside to give him enough room to enter.

It was dark and creepy inside the empty classroom. No chairs or a sign of a teacher's desk. He went to the classroom door and opened it. It made a loud creaking noise, which echoed through the school.

Michael walked into the hallway. Only small cracks of the moonlit sky found a way in. With the little bit of light he had, Michael walked down the hallway. He started to venture around, hearing nothing but his own footsteps. This isn't really that bad, Michael thought. I don't know what everyone is so scared about. He looked into each classroom. They were all dark and empty. Well I think I've been here long enough. I think I've showed those guys that I wasn't scared. Just then Michael heard a noise. It seemed to come from behind a door at the end of the hall.

This door was further than the others. He walked quickly down the hallway and arrived at the mysterious door. He slowly opened it. This was not a classroom, but a long narrow hallway.

There was no way that he wanted to go through and sec where the hallway led. But Michael felt curious when he saw a light that shined in the distance. He walked down the hallway and entered into another room.

The room was surrounded by old rusted pipes, which led to a giant furnace. Michael walked past the giant furnace and came to a dusty wooden workbench. The bench was cluttered with books, tools, and a large metal axe.

His eyes also caught something else. There on the workbench was a broken and dirty ashtray. On the edge of the astray laid a single cigarette, it was slowly burning away.

Seeing the lit cigarette, Michael was scared. He looked around the room to see if anyone was watching him. He looked to his right, left, and then up.

His jaw slowly opened, as his eyes widened in disbelief. There on the ceiling he saw dozens of dead carcasses hanging off of different size hooks.

Back down the darkened passageway he ran. Out of the door and back into the main hallway. He continued to run, but had forgotten which classroom door he had first come out of. Michael ran down one hallway, then another, but each classroom door looked the same.

Michael ran as fast as he could, as the noises from his footsteps echoed through the school. He didn't want to, but he had to stop to catch his breath. He huffed out from his tired lungs and listened. The sounds of footsteps did not stop, and they seemed to be getting closer.

He walked quickly with all the energy that he had left. He turned right and saw a pair of doors that lead to the outside. The hallway was long, but he knew he could make it.

Michael picked up speed and prayed that the doors were not locked. The sounds of the footsteps behind him sounded if they had gotten closer than before. He started to run harder. Michael had a feeling that he was racing for only one thing, his young life.

He reached the doors and gave them a hard shove. The doors swung open with ease.

"There he is." One of Brad's friends said and started to laugh with the others.

Michael, still breathing heavily, saw Brad's friends laughing in front of him. Before he could say anything, he felt a hand grab his shoulder. The fear hit him hard, as his heart beaten too fast for him to catch his breath. Michael turned around to see Brad gleaming with a big white smile.

"Can't scare the new kid, huh?" Brad asked as he started to laugh along with his friends.

Michael backed away, when he saw a gruesome-looking figure come out from the school. He tried to warn Brad, but couldn't open his mouth in time. All he could do was watch. Watch as the gruesome man's axe came swinging down across Brad's waist. Blood poured out of his mouth, as he stood there still laughing at Michael.

Brad's friends' screamed and grabbed Michael before he became the next victim.

"Louis," someone shouted. "How many times have I told you not to leave the school?"

Louis lowered the bloody axe and made a small whimper sound in front of Joy.

"Come on, I'll help you clean up this mess, but no more," Joy said as she helped her brother clean up Brad's lifeless body.

Later that night in the back room of the old school, Louis sat there cleaning his axe, as he tried whistling to a small tune. Far back into the dark corner, hanging from an old rusted hook, was Brad's blood-soaked head.

He Needs Body Parts

If anyone had asked Sammy's parents about their son, they would say that Sammy was a very creative and intelligent 10-year-old boy. Who would do the normal boyhood things; Play ball, ride his bicycle, or just hang around. Hanging around was one of those things that his parents did not approve of. Not that he hung out, but where.

Sammy spent most of his summer days in the town's cemetery. It looked quite old to him and seemed not very well taking care of. The grass was overgrown, the trees and bushes never seemed to be trimmed. But that's what Sammy like about it. The cemetery looked spooky, and he felt it was the perfect place to write his scary ghost stories. Sammy would sit there for hours and write the most imaginative stories. Then around dusk he would walk back home and in the morning he would tell these stories to his parents.

At first, the stories made his parents concerned about his strange imagination. But after a while, his parents would just laugh off his weird stories and hoped that it was just a phase.

One day, Sammy came home and told his parents about a tall thin man he had seen in the cemetery. The man arrived just after dusk and started to dig up coffins. He dragged out the corpses and then chopped off different body parts using a very large axe.

His parents thought it was one of his crazy ghost stories, but Sammy tried to explain that he wasn't making this one up. It was the truth. His parents still did not believe him.

Sammy went back to the gravesite where he had seen the tall man before. "Maybe if they had came back with me, I could have proved that I wasn't making it up," Sammy said out loud.

Upon his arrival, all the graves that had been disturbed were now covered back up. "They won't believe me now if there is nothing for them to see." Sammy decided to wait until tomorrow to revisit the cemetery.

When dusk came the following day, Sammy sneaked out of his house and returned to the cemetery. Again, he saw the tall man hacking off body parts and he threw them into a large black bag.

Sammy felt he needed to prove to his parents that this man was real, and not his imagination. He decided to come back again, but this time with a camera. It might be the only way his parents would ever believe him.

The next morning, the family sat at the breakfast table. This is usually when Sammy told his ghoulish stories, but he was not in the mood today. He sat there quietly and read the back of his cereal box.

"Could I be excused?" Sammy asked.

"Sammy, you hardly touched your breakfast." His Mother answered.

"I know, but there's this toy I want to buy today," Sammy lied. He never liked to lie to his parents, but he felt this time he had to.

His father sighed and looked at him. "You never have money. What happened, did you rob a bank?"

"No, I've been saving." That wasn't a lie. Sammy had been saving for a remote control car for some time now. But he felt buying a camera was more important.

"What's the point of saving your money, if you're going to go out and spend it?" His dad asked.

"But that's the reason I was saving my money, to buy this one toy." Sammy tried to explain.

"Go ahead, Sammy." his mother said, and Sammy left the table, and ran to the garage to get his bicycle.

A disposable camera was all Sammy could afford. He raced home and brought the camera up to his room. He read all the directions, which were printed on the camera. Sammy took a sample shot of his room to get an idea on how to use it. Then waited that night to sneak out of the house.

When the dusk settled across the sky, Sammy sneaked out and ran to the cemetery, back to the tombstones where he had seen the tall man before. The man was not there, the dirt below the tombstones have not even been touched. Then Sammy heard a noise a few yards from him. It was the tall man.

The man was there looking in other caskets. Sammy watched him as he shuffled through the different body parts. It almost seemed that the tall man couldn't find what he was looking for. Coffin after coffin, he opened and threw the lid back down.

This was Sammy's chance to get it on film. He sunk down between two headstones so that the man would not see him, took out his camera and aimed it at the tall man. There was one thing that Sammy didn't realize would happen. The camera had flashed when he took the picture.

Sammy ran home and never looked back. He did not know if the tall man saw him or not. When Sammy got home and told his parents the news about the cemetery, he found his parents yelling at him for sneaking out.

"Sam, I've had enough of your stories!" his father scolded. "I should have said this before, but no more! No more stories, no more going out at night, and you are not allowed to set foot into that cemetery. Never, you got me?"

Sammy showed them the camera, but his mother grabbed it out of his hands and sent him to his room.

In the bedroom, Sammy looked out the window and cried because his parents didn't believe him. He looked out to the darkened street in front of his house. The single streetlight shined onto the dark pavement, he sat and watched as the moths circled around the glow of the light.

Sammy's watery eyes caught something else. He looked down and there out from the shadows was the tall man. The man walked underneath the streetlight and then stopped. Sammy noticed the man was carrying a black bag and a very large axe.

The tall man turned his head and looked up into Sammy's window, then waved. Sammy ran to his bedroom door, locked it and hid beneath the covers.

When Sammy awoke in the morning, he climbed out of his bed and unlocked his bedroom door. He slowly walked down to the kitchen to find his mother. She was not there. But Sammy found tracks of mud on the kitchen floor. He followed the tracks of mud down into the next room.

There in the living room, sitting in the middle of the floor, Sammy saw his parents. They had been gagged and tied together. His mother looked up at Sammy with great pain in her eyes. A pool of blood surrounded them. Sammy noticed his mother was missing her left ring finger, his father was missing both of his eyes.

"Do you believe me now?" Sammy asked.

How To Write A Horror Novel

It was the night before Christmas, and all was silent in the deepest part of the North Pole. The unpolluted white snow melted beneath the warm red blood. All eight of his reindeer have been slashed open and gutted. Santa could only look in horror at his devoted animals. They worked so hard for him on this special night. Never again will he be able to say the words: Come on, Blitzen, Prancer, away. He felt the freezing hail rake at his rosy nose. The clock in his head rang 11:58. He was late. Santa Claus feared for his life. The elves were out tonight and angered with vengeance.

Jill Styles stopped reading in the middle of the page and looked up to where Martin Wells was sitting. His smile rose from ear to ear with delight.

"So what do you think?" Martin asked excitedly. "I think I could see something like that published."

"Martin," Jill responded. "I don't think the reading world is ready for killer elves. Besides, I thought you were a sports writer."

"I'm sick of writing for the newspaper." He got up and paced around Jill's office. "I want to venture out, be creative and damn it, write the best horror story ever." Martin stopped in front of Jill and placed his hands on her desk. "You're the publisher. Can't you help me out?" He asked as he looked into her bright green eyes.

"You know, horror doesn't sell that well," Jill said as she flipped through the pages of his story.

"Don't give me that." Martin became annoyed, as he sat back down in the vinyl chair. "Please. Be honest with me."

"Okay, it's the story. The writing itself is amazing, but the story falls flat. It's phony."

"It's fiction."

"Martin," she stopped and took a deep breath. "Look, I hope you don't take this the wrong way. Maybe writing a horror novel is not for you."

"Please, Jill," he pleaded with her. "Is there any way you can help me?"

Jill stayed silent for a moment, got up from where she was sitting and glided to her office door to close it. She went back to Martin and leaned back against her desk. “Okay, we’re about to publish a new writer named Nancy Cornetta. She sent me the scariest manuscript that I’ve ever read. I’m not allowed to give out any details about it, but let’s just say that I can never go camping again.”

“Are you rubbing in on how bad my story is?”

“No, but I think she can help you. I never do this, but because you’re a personal friend of mine, I will give you her number.” She went back behind her desk and pulled out her card file. Jill flipped through the cards until she came to Nancy’s. “Here you go. Give her a call.”

“What, call her and then what, she’ll become my co-author?”

“Not exactly. Just find out how she does it, how she makes her stories seem so realistic and scary.” Jill handed over Nancy’s card.

It took fifty-two hours for Martin to call Nancy Cornetta. At first, he didn’t think he needed help. But he read over his elf story again and again. He realized it could be better. Much better.

His telephone conversation with Nancy was short and to the point. The tone of her voice was pleasant, and she seemed willing to help. Martin wanted to ask her questions over the phone, but Nancy asked him to meet her instead. He agreed to meet her the following night.

The Cabin’s Claw was right outside of O’Hare airport. It was known as a pick-up bar for people who would only be in town for a few days. Martin walked in a little later than expected. He saw Nancy sitting at a table near the end of the bar. Her hair was light blonde, and long. The blue dress she wore sparkled beneath the bright lights of the bar. Nancy looked the way she said she would over the telephone.

"Hello, Nancy. I'm Martin."

Nancy said hello and watched him sit down. She noticed the light gray suit he was wearing, and a black shirt underneath. She thought he looked to be in his late 40's. But it was hard to tell. Not many people at that age shave their head. She noticed that he didn't have an impatient look in his face, so he might be without kids and possibly single.

"What kind of stories do you write?" Nancy got right down to business.

"Nothing yet." Martin felt too embarrassed to tell her about his killer elf story. "But, I'd like to get into the horror field."

"Horror, like a science fiction story where little green men invade earth? Or maybe something in the line of ghosts that haunt a medieval castle?"

"Nothing that far out of reach. I was thinking more about a deranged killer, a stalker on the prowl."

"A stalker?" She sounded interested. "Why would this person be stalking?"

Martin didn't know why. All this was new to him. He never asked these questions to himself. Although he had never seen Nancy's work, he had a feeling she was pretty good at this. "He stalks redheads, so you should be lucky you're a blonde."

"He's a stalker who likes to hunt redheads." Nancy gazed around the room and saw the young female sitting across from them. She had long, curly red hair. "Good choice," she said and turned back to Martin. "Now, what would your stalker do?"

"He would kill her."

"Why?"

"Because she's a red head," he answered.

"What is he prejudiced against women with red hair?"

"No, it's just what he's into. That's who he likes to stalk."

"But why? There must be a reason."

"True. Because he once got fired from his boss, who was also a redhead." Martin tried to picture it in his head.

"Do you have anything better?" she asked.

"Because he thinks all redheads are evil, and they should be stalked and killed."

"I'm with you. Now what is he going to kill her with?"

They looked at the redheaded woman. She sat alone with a drink in her hand.

"He could strangle her. He could strangle her with his bare hands." Martin started to feel a part of something, part of a great book.

"I don't know. She looks pretty fast. She might outrun him."

"Okay, how about a gun?"

"Where would he get it?"

"A gun store," Martin suggested, as he began to feel unsure of himself now.

"Ouch!" Nancy let out. "Let's see, the police match the bullet to the gun. The gun is registered under his name. He's not a very smart homicidal maniac, is he?"

"Forget the gun," he shouted.

"How about an axe?" She suggested. "I think there's nothing sexier than an axe murderer."

"An axe it is then," Martin agreed.

"So your stalker goes over there and kills her with an axe?"

"You lost me."

"How would he bring the axe into the bar in the first place?" Nancy asked. "I don't think they'd allow that in here."

"That's true." He was starting to get the idea. "You see he's a very patient individual. He would wait here as long as he had to. He would watch his prey, and when she leaves, he'll leave. He would follow her all the way home."

"Creepy."

"Do you think so?"

"Uh-oh!"

"What, you don't like the idea?" He needed to know.

"Your redhead is leaving."

"So?"

"So? She's getting away." Nancy tugged on Martin's sleeve. "Your axe murderer wouldn't just sit here."

"What, you want me to go follow her?" Martin asked, thinking she was joking.

"Yes, you said you wanted to write a horror story, so now I'm going to show you how to."

They left the bar and entered the parking lot. Martin saw the redheaded woman open the door to a yellow Jeep.

"There she is," he told Nancy.

"Who's driving?" she questioned.

"My car is right here." He pointed to his white 1998 Explorer. "Here, you drive. I want to start writing this down." He handed her the keys to his trunk and got into the passenger side.

Nancy followed the young redhead in her yellow jeep, as Martin took out his little green writing pad that he kept inside his suit jacket.

Before Martin was done writing, he looked up to see Nancy pulling to the curb. He looked across the street to see a dark blue house. There in the driveway the yellow jeep was parked. The redheaded woman exited the jeep and opened the garage door to her house.

"I wonder if she always keeps her garage door unlocked?"

"Do you think she noticed us?" Martin asked as he continued to watch the young woman park her jeep inside the garage.

"No, but I think someone else has." Nancy pointed to a man who was walking his dog and staring at the Ford Explorer. "When you're an axe murderer, you can never be too careful." She stepped on the gas and drove away from the house.

Martin started to laugh. “I can’t believe we did this. We followed someone home. We actually stalked someone. That was a lot of fun.”

“It’s not over yet. What if the guy with the dog wasn’t there? What would the stalker’s next move be?” She watched as he flipped through his notes. “The reason we followed her home was for you to get a feel of what your stalker would do.”

“He would take out his axe, which he keeps in the truck.”

“Would he kill her tonight, or would he just watch her? Watch her every move through the darkened windows.”

“I believe he would kill her tonight.”

“How would he get into the house, supposing she locks the garage door behind her?”

“He wouldn’t have to. He would kill her in the garage before she has a chance to close it. She would think she was nice and safe after she parked her jeep for the night. The stalker would sneak up on her, and when she got out. He would go for the kill, whack her to death before she even knew what was happening.”

“I like killers like that,” Nancy said and smiled at him. “They get right to the point.”

After Martin said good-bye and thanked Nancy, he drove home from the Cabin’s Claw to work on his new book. His brain was exploding from ideas about his axe-murdering stalker. When he arrived home, he typed for hours, then days, only taking breaks to eat and sleep.

For four days, Martin sat and typed out his story. Every half-hour that went by, he saved his work on his computer. He would type some more, than would save it in the computer file he named "Stalker". But that evening, he was interrupted by the annoying sound of the telephone. He felt very disturbed to be away from his work to answer it, but he did. "Hello?"

"Hello," a female voice answered back. "How's the story coming?"

"Nancy, you would be so proud of me." He was happy to hear from her again.

"Do you mind if I read what you have so far?"

At first he hesitated, but without her there would be no inspiration for a story. "Do you know a place called Arthur's?" Martin asked. "It's a little closer to me than the Cabin's Claw."

"I'll meet you there. I'm leaving now. Bye."

Martin hung up the phone, went into the bathroom and washed his face. He knew he hadn't taken a shower in days. But all he needed was some deodorant and a clean shirt.

Once they were at Arthur's, Nancy skimmed through Martin's pages of work. He sat there with a beer in his hand.

"Huh?"

"You don't like it?" He was surprised.

"Well, you have two killings in here."

"Yes, they're both redheads. I have the first one killed in the garage, and the other is by the pool."

"I see that. I'm just saying they seem too similar. Not the pool and garage, but the way they got killed. Just seems so plain. You should try and mix it up a little bit."

"I see."

"You have here that he was walking by, saw the redhead swimming, ran to his truck, got his axe and went back to kill her. I think you can be more creative than that."

"She was on the way to the pool."

"Listen, he stalked the first girl at the bar, so keep it in bars. Make that his private hunting ground."

"Good idea."

"Let's say that that woman over there is a redhead." Nancy pointed to a brunette who is by the jukebox and picking out songs to play.

"So he'll wait here and watch her."

"No, he's already done that. Let us make him more eager this time. Let's say he goes up to her and starts talking."

"You think he would do that?" Martin was unsure.

"Of course. Think about it. He has already killed once, but now he wants more out of it. He wants to understand these red-headed devils a little closer."

"I got it." he smiled at Nancy as he took out his little green notepad.

"Let's go."

"Go where?"

"We need to talk to his next victim."

"Are you serious?" Martin asked. "Of course you're serious. Let's go talk to her." He followed Nancy over to the girl at the jukebox.

"Hello," Nancy said. "This is my friend Martin."

"Hello," Martin said shyly.

"Hey," the girl answered back, still looking for a song to play.

"Martin was just telling me how much he loves your hair," Nancy said.

"Uh-huh," she responded, pressing the number sequence for the song she picked. A slow blues tune rang out from the bar's speakers.

"Would you like to dance?" Martin asked the girl.

"Get lost," the girl said, walking away.

Martin felt annoyed. "Well got to go," he said and turned to leave.

"No, this is good," Nancy assured him.

"How's this good?" he asked. "I just got turned down by a woman that I wasn't even interested in."

"Yes, but now you know how the stalker would feel if he was interested," she explained. "How do you feel now?"

"I want to kill her. I wouldn't even wait until she got home. I would go out and kill her in the parking lot."

"That's real good Martin. Go home and write that." Nancy gave him back his pages and watched him leave.

Four days and three drafts later, Martin felt excited about his work. He could not wait to show the world what he had written. When the telephone rang this time, he didn't mind it as much.

"How are you doing," Nancy didn't wait for him to say hello this time.

"Excellent. I have about two more pages to go."

"Can I take a peek at it?"

"You sure can."

Nancy met Martin at his place this time and read his story from the first page to the last.

"Wow, I'm impressed."

"Really? You think it's that good?" He was happy to please her, and he could not wait to turn the story over to Jill to have it published.

"Yes, although…"

"What's wrong now?" He thought the story was perfect.

"I had a hard time with the ending," she said, looking back into Martin's green eyes.

"Well, you see, he finds the perfect redhead and falls in love with her," he explains, "and after he sleeps with her, he realizes that he can't stop himself from his killing spree."

"I understood that part. It was the sex scene I had trouble with."

"Oh!" Martin said, as his cheeks turned red.

"Hold on." Nancy walked out of the room with her purse. When she returned she was wearing a black silk nightgown and a red wig. "What would the stalker do with me?" Nancy asked, leading him into his bedroom.

They role-played in his bed for two hours that night. Martin understood the energy the stalker had in the bedroom. He didn't need to write this night down in his little green notepad to remember.

Nancy was gone by the time Martin dragged himself out of bed. He turned on his computer to start writing, but his story was not there. Neither was his manuscript. His notebook wasn't in his jacket pocket. Furious, he grabbed the phone. Before he could punch in Nancy's number, there was a knock at his door. Martin opened it to see the police in front of him.

"I'm Detective Goodman." A man dressed in a brown suit stepped in front of Martin's doorway. "Is that your Ford Explorer out front?"

"Yes," Martin answered back, looking over at his truck. The police were opening the doors and starting to search it. "May I ask what's going on here?"

The detective took a stack of pictures from his jacket and showed one to Martin. A dark blue house stood in the frame. "A neighbor said he spotted a car like yours in front of this house on August 9th."

"Well, yes, but I was working on a project."

The detective showed him the next picture he had. It was a picture of the brunette he had seen at the jukebox. "I have eyewitnesses who saw you talking with this girl at a place called Arthur's on August 13th."

"She turned me down," Martin laughed to himself. "I still don't see a point to all this?"

"Whether you are aware of this or not, Mr. Wells, both of these women have been murdered."

Martin's mouth dropped. He was speechless.

"Is this yours?" The detective asked, holding up Martin's green notepad.

Martin nodded.

"Then I guess you are already aware of this," the detective continued. "Each murder is identical to the way you have it written in here. The first Victim was murdered in her garage on August 10th, and the second victim was murdered in the parking lot on August 13th, just a few hours after you were seen talking to her."

"I didn't do a thing."

"Detective, take a look at this," one of the police officers shouted, after looking into the back of Martin's truck. "It's an axe."

Detective Goodman looked back at Martin. "You have the right to remain silent."

She was sitting down at her computer and retyped the title of the book. "The Stalker. By Nancy Cornetta." Nancy tapped the print button on her computer. "Jill will be happy with this one."

I Will Never Let You Go

I see you every day, but I still can't talk to you the way I want to. I'm just too afraid. You paralyze me.

When I'm all alone crying in the dark, all I want to do is scream out your name. You're a caring person. I know this. I see how you treat people, and I love that about you. I watch as you head in my direction. I sense your eyes looking into my soul. I want to tell you how much I love you. But if you knew I watched you every night, you would think of me as a freak.

The waitress walked up to the booth where Stanley Miller was sitting.

"Good morning, would you like some coffee this morning?" Mary Barkley asked. She had a soft spot for this customer. He came in every morning, sits in the same booth and orders the same meal, eggs on toast.

"Yes, please." Stanley responded in a shy tone. Please tell me that you love me, he thought.

"Would you like your usual?"

"Yes, please," he said again. How could I tell her that I stare through her window at night? One day I hope you will be mine. If you could only look beyond my flesh and see what was in my heart, I know you would love me back.

Stanley watched her walk to the cook to place his order. Her short blonde hair and beautiful blue eyes were still in his head. His thoughts disappeared when the front door to the coffee shop opened. Stanley saw his most hated enemy. Officer Adam Davis, the most handsome cop in town.

Stanley knew Adam from high school. Stanley would always be teased for his slowness and the special classes he attended. Stanley knew he could never be as popular as Adam. But what he hated most about Adam was that he was dating the most beautiful girl in the world. Mary Barkley.

As he watched the two kiss each other hello, Stanley tightened his hand around a paper napkin and ripped it to pieces. Why him? What makes him so special? What about the other people who have no one in our world? Just once I want to take her into my arms and never let her go.

"Adam, stop it." Mary shouted, as he started to tickle her. "I have to go back to work!"

"Are you coming over tonight?" Adam asked with a sneaky grin upon his face.

"Mary, pick up!" The cook called.

"I can't. I have too much work to do at home," she explained to Adam. "My apartment is a mess."

"Well, I can help you clean the floor," Adam teased.

"Adam, no." She walked over and took the tray of food to the booth where Stanley had been sitting. Mary looked around the shop, but he was nowhere in sight. She looked back down at the table and saw a five-dollar tip that he left for her.

"Are you okay, dear?" Adam questioned as he came up from behind her.

"Idiot!" Stanley spoke to himself. "Why didn't I say anything to her, and why didn't I stop that rat from touching here? I can treat her better than that. But no, I left with my tail between my legs. Things will be different. I'll show her that I can take her into my arms and will never let her go."

It was 4:58 on a Friday morning. The November rain hit the window of the small apartment. Mary slept peacefully in her cozy bed. She went to sleep quite early last night. She knew she had to be at the coffee shop at 6:00. It was usually busy on Fridays, but Mary didn't mind. Her regular customers were always good to her, and they knew they would get their usual meal without asking her first.

At 5:00, the alarm on her clock sang its morning tune. She felt too tired to get up, but she knew she had to. With her eyes still closed, she sat up and reached for her alarm clock. A cold wet hand grabbed her arm. Mary's eyes sprung open and she saw a man standing in front of her.

"What are you doing here?" Mary yelled. "What, you like watching me sleep? You are a sick pervert, get out of here!"

The man didn't move.

"Fine." Mary said. She went to get up from her bed, but the man threw her back down. He climbed on top of her and started to kiss her neck. Mary tried to get him off of her. She squirmed left and right, but he was too heavy for her to budge. His hands rubbed against her upper body and then down to her legs.

"Adam, this isn't funny," she said.

"Come on, I'm only playing with you babe." Adam loosened his grip.

"Maybe if you came here an hour earlier, we could have done something."

"So call in late." He started to kiss her neck again.

"Adam, I'm sorry. I can't." She apologized.

As Adam got up from the bed, they heard the building's fire alarm start to ring.

"What is that?" Mary asked nervously.

Without answering her back, Adam ran to the door that led into the hallway. He opened the door to see a man, the man was dripping wet and holding a fire axe in his hands.

Eight minutes later, the first team of firemen reached the apartment building.

"I'll check the first floor, you and Charlie check the second." The fire chief said to his two co-workers.

The fire chief entered the hallway on the first floor, he noticed broken glass scattered around the floor. Above the broken glass was a box where the fire axe was located. Now missing, he cautiously continued down the hallway and came to an open door.

The fire chief made his way into the apartment, he checked each room as he announced himself. When he reached the bedroom he saw his good friend, Officer Adam Davis, soaked in blood. His body had been laid next to another corpse. Their head was missing.

Stanley sat by the railroad tracks, stroking Mary's short blonde hair. He crooned the same words over and over. "I will never let you go."

Cabin With A View

"Wouldn't it be great if we could rent a place like that?" Ann asked her husband Jeff.

"Are we not on our way to the cabin that we rented?"

"Yes, but look at it. The one we rented looks nothing like that." Ann pointed back to the tall cabin. The view on the back was the sight Ann notice first. Glass windows covered the entire side down to a glass door. The door opened onto a wide deck hanging over the steep edge of the mountain.

"Sure, we'll just go up there and invite ourselves in," Jeff said as he continued driving.

"No, but we can ask if they would like to rent it to us."

"Are you serious?"

"You own a real estate business. Use your charm," Ann demanded. "The worst they can say is no."

"What are we going to do about the cabin we're headed to?" Jeff asked.

"Let your brother use it."

"You know my brother. He's not going to come all the way from Jersey to rent a cabin."

"If it's free, he will." She assured him.

"You expect me to pay for both of them?"

"It's for our anniversary," she pleaded with him.

Jeff turned his Mercedes around and headed back to the cabin with the great high deck. He drove the car up the stone-filled driveway and parked in front of the cabin.

"I want to see the deck first," Ann said running to the back of the cabin, with Jeff close behind.

Their eyes followed the thin wooded stilts that held the large deck high above them.

"That must be 30 feet high," Jeff said in amazement.

"Thirty-four, to be exact." Said a voice behind them.

The couple turned to see a man who looked to be in his late thirties. He was dressed in a flannel shirt and wore a pair of blue jeans.

"We're sorry. We didn't mean to be trespassing." Ann said apologetically.

"That's okay." The man said, placing his hands inside his pockets. "Try not to get too close to the edge there."

Jeff looked and saw the far rocky drop behind him. He looked back at the man and asked Ann's request. "I know this might sound crazy, but we were wondering if you might be interested in renting your cabin?"

"What, today?" The man jokingly replied.

"Whenever you possibly could. You see, my wife Ann and I, saw your cabin and thought we might ask about it."

"I never rented out a home before. I wouldn't even know where to start."

"If it helps, I'm in the real estate business." Jeff explained. "I can take care of any paperwork you may need, plus a list of the current market analysis.

"That's very nice, really. But I just feel a bit strange offering my place to people that I don't know."

"My name is Jeff, and this is my wife Ann." They both smiled at him.

"Hello, I'm Derek. I would introduce you to my wife, but she's in Sweden at the moment."

"Oh, how wonderful." Ann said.

"Yes, actually, I'll be flying out there tomorrow morning. First class." Derek threw in. He'd seen the Mercedes when they pulled into his driveway. "So I really won't have time to go through any paperwork. I'm sorry."

"We love your deck." Ann spoke again.

"Thank you, we just had it put in about three weeks ago. The neighbors seem to be a little jealous of it, but we like it."

"Tell you what, think it over," Jeff said, pulling out his business card and wrote on the back of it. "If you change your mind, give me a call on my cell phone."

"Will do."

Derek watched as the couple left in their Mercedes. He flipped over the card and read the back. One weekend: 2,500 a night. Derek was amazed at the price.

The next morning Derek decided to called Jeff about the offer on the house. "Hello, Jeff, Derek Johnson here. I've been thinking about your offer, and I've decided to take you up on it. I'll leave the keys in the mailbox and fresh towels on the bed."

Later that day Jeff and Ann drove up to the cabin. The keys were left in the mailbox as promised. They couldn't imagine a better place for their anniversary.

The high ceiling showed all three rooms in the tall cabin. In the large living room, two sofas sat across from each other, as a statue of a black panther held up a glass coffee table. The kitchen was connected to the living room as an island bar separated the two rooms. Next to the kitchen was a small bathroom with a stand-up shower. A wooden ladder led to the only bedroom, which hung over the living room. Connected to the bedroom was a small flight of stairs. They climbed the steps to a glass door, and opened it.

Jeff and Ann stepped out onto the large wooden deck. It was a beautiful sight they saw. Acres and acres of land covered their view. The mountains and trees seemed endless.

"Look at this view." Jeff was amazed.

"How high do you think we are?"

Jeff looked down and almost lost his balance from the shock of the height. He knew that the deck itself was 34 feet, but adding the cliff that the deck hung off of, was extremely high.

"I'm guessing at least 200 feet."

As the dusk developed into night Jeff poured red wine into a glass for Ann. They cuddled up next to each other on the king-sized bed. It was peaceful, and just what they needed.

Suddenly a strange noise came from outside, it startled them both.

"What was that?" Ann jumped and looked at Jeff.

"Stay here," he told her and went out to investigate the noise. Jeff opened the glass door and the noise stopped. It was too dark for him to see much of anything, and all he could hear was the howling of the wind.

He went back inside thinking nothing of the sounds, and rejoined Ann. He looked deep into her eyes and whispered that he loved her. As he started to kiss her soft lips, the noises started again. Jeff and Ann could not figure out what it was, but the sound was loud, and echoing around them.

"Maybe the wind is hitting something against the house," Ann suggested pulling the blanket around her.

"Let me check it out again," Jeff said and stepped back outside onto the deck. He looked over the edge and the noise stopped. It was still too dark for him to see. "Where is the moonlight when you need it?" he said to himself.

Jeff turned around and headed back inside. The noise started up immediately. He entered the bedroom and started to search around for a flashlight.

"What are you doing?" Ann asked.

"Looking to see if they have a flashlight." Jeff answered back as he opened a closet door.

"They probably have one in the kitchen." Ann said, then got out of bed and climbed down the ladder to the next level.

Jeff abandoned his search for the flashlight, and walked back to the glass door and opened it. Before he could step out onto the deck, Ann quickly walked up behind him with a flashlight in her hand.

"Stay here," he said, as he tried to take the flashlight from her.

"No, I want to go with you." She said, tightly holding onto the flashlight.

"Fine, but stay close."

Jeff and Ann walked slowly onto the deck. With the weight of their bodies combined, the deck went crashing down onto the rocks far below.

"Good job, dad!" Dave's son shouted.

"I told those damn Johnson's if they built that thing on my side of the property line, I was going to chop it down."

"I'm surprised they're not coming out here and yelling at us."

"They're in Sweden right now. Won't they be in for a surprise when they come home?"

Dave picked up his axe and carried it on his shoulder. He looked down at his son and smiled. "Let's go home."

Shame On The Night

Ashley almost couldn't see the road in front of her, as the rain poured heavily against the windshield of her '76 Duster. Diane sat in the passenger side and lowered the radio as the song, "Don't Fear The Reaper." faded.

"That was one of the worst parties Steve had ever thrown," Diane complained as she fiddled with her wavy blonde hair in the visor mirror.

"Nothing can top last year's party," Ashley remarked. "And he didn't even have a band this time."

"Yeah, right," Diane said, looking outside of her window into the dark wilderness. "It's almost two in the morning, and I'm bored out of my mind."

"Relax, we're almost back at the dorm." Sometimes, Ashley wondered if she should be more outgoing like Diane. She thought she was attractive, but more in a conservative way. Although she might not tease her long brown hair the way Diane did. She liked it straight and simple. Ashley asked herself why Diane had the majority of dates between the two of them. What did Diane have that she didn't?

"What am I supposed to do there, light fireworks or something?" Diane joked.

"Why don't you give George a call? He should be up."

"He's lame. You can have him."

"I don't want your leftovers," Ashley said rudely. "And I'm sorry you're bored, but I'm tired. I can't see anything, and if you can find something to do while we drive down this empty road, be my guest."

"Anything?" Diane questioned.

"Whatever you want Diane."

"I want to pick up that hitchhiker," and pointed to the man who was standing on the side of the road.

Ashley didn't know how she saw the man, as he stood there in the rain. He wore a yellow raincoat and held his thumb up into the air.

"I don't think so," Ashley said seriously.

"You said anything. Besides, he looks cute."

"How can you tell? I can hardly see him in this rain."

"Please, Ashley, it will be fun. I'll let you borrow my black mini skirt that you keep on nagging me about."

"Fine, but if he looks dangerous, I'm speeding away."

She slowed the car down a few feet away from the man. Diane rolled down the window.

"Hey, do you need a ride?"

The man walked quickly over to their car and looked through the window at the two girls. He was a lot cuter than Ashley expected. She cursed Diane in her head for always finding the good-looking ones.

"Thanks," the man said, as they let him into the back seat. "I'm surprised that you girls stopped," he said in a deep Irish accent.

"We like helping out our fellow man," Diane said with a giggle in her voice.

"It was my idea." Ashley jumped in.

Diane gave Ashley a dirty look, and then turned her attention to their new passenger. "Where are you headed on this dark and stormy night?"

"The Train station, if you could," the man said.

"Not a problem," Ashley continued. "What's your name?"

"Charlie," he said, removing his raincoat.

"Hey, Charlie, I'm Diane and this loose goose over here is Ashley."

"Hello, Charlie," Ashley said cheerfully. "So, why were you surprised that two sweet girls wanted to give you a ride?"

"I didn't think I would get a chance from anyone. Especially with all these roadside killings lately."

The two girls looked at each other, knowing that they never heard those rumors. Diane looked back over at Charlie. "What killings?"

"There's a lunatic out there, and he only comes out at night."

"Maybe because his day job is not as flexible as he would like it to be," Diane joked.

"He hitchhikes, up and down this road." Charlie continued. "If you were unlucky enough to pick him up, he put a small slash in your tire. Then a few miles down the road, you have to pull over to change it. That's when he would strike."

"Are you putting us on?" Ashley asked, looking at Charlie through the rear view mirror.

"I wish I was, but it wasn't only hitchhiking. He did other things to lure his victims in. Sometimes he wave them down and say that he was just in a car accident. Or that he lost his little girl in the woods. The ones that followed him were the ones that never came out alive."

"What's the worst story you have heard about this man?" Diane asked.

"There are quite a few of them."

"Just give us your top three that you've heard."

"Okay, girls, but let me tell you that they're not very pleasant." Charlie leaned closer to the girls and lowered his voice to a creepy tone. "One time, he hid in back of a woman's car and waited for her to return. The woman left late from the church where she was playing bingo that night. She drove all the way home, not knowing there was a stranger in the back seat. When she reached her driveway, he popped up and stuck a hunting knife at her throat. He told her that all he wanted was the valuables in the house and he'll leave without hurting anyone. He lied. The crazed man killed her, her husband, and their two small kids."

"Oh my God!" Ashley covered her mouth as she listened to his terrifying words.

"I don't know if I should go on. The stories do get worse," he said, smoothing down the top of his brown wet hair.

"I'm not scared yet," Diane said proudly.

"There was a young girl, about the same age as both of you." He continued, "she was at party, she felt too drunk to drive, so she decided to walk home. Not a wise thing to do at two o'clock in the morning."

"What happened to her?" Ashley asked.

"Have you ever seen those old black and white movies where the villain ties up the woman across the railroad tracks?"

Both girls answered yes, and Charlie continued.

"Very similar, but what he would do was just tie her ankles across one of the tracks. He would stay and watch as the train cut through her legs. From there, he dragged her across the gravel of stones and onto a second track, the express track."

"Why would he do that?" Diane asked.

"It's not an easy task to move without your feet. Plus, the rest of her legs would start to become numb. He wanted to see if she could escape from the tracks before the next train came."

"Did she?" The girls asked.

"She was close, but no awards are given out for second place when you're matched up against an express line."

"This is a very sick individual," Ashley exclaimed.

"No kidding," Diane responded.

"That wasn't the worst story," he said, leaning his head back against the seat. "I really don't believe you want to hear the next one. Not only is it gruesome, it's perverted and just plain horrible."

"I need to hear it," Diane stated. "Don't ask me why. Something tells me not to. But the more I know, the less I'll go to parties and pick up strange men."

"It's not pretty." Charlie cleared his throat and began the story. "It involved these two college girls that had just left a party. On their way home, they picked up this hitchhiker. They thought it would be a nice thing to do. Our crazed man asked them their names, what school they were going to, their dorm number, everything."

"I would be freaked out if someone asked me all those questions," Ashley said.

"They didn't think anything of it. But then, on Christmas Eve, he broke into their dorm room as they slept peacefully in their beds. He yanked each girl out, tied them down to the floor and left."

"He left them there?" Diane asked. "No one would find the girls until the holiday season was over."

"No, he returned the following night. He entered the dorm room wearing a ski mask over his head and had a video camera in his hand. For the next three nights, he tortured and fondled each student while he taped each perverted stunt."

"Oh my God," Ashley whispered out again.

"He ransacked their dorm room and found an address book. He made copies of the tape and mailed them to the girls' boyfriends and their family members. But before he left on that last day, he set up a device. He tied a long piece of rope from the door to the ceiling. The rope from the ceiling held two axes that hung over the girls' necks. When the police received a call from one of the recipients of the tape. The officers went to check on the girls and went to their dorm room. As they opened the door, the two axes plummeted down and chopped off their heads."

"I'm getting chills just thinking about it," Ashley stammered. "Where did you get all these details?"

"I'm a journalist. Been following this story for months."

"The police haven't found him yet?" Diane asked.

"No, he's still out there, stalking the night."

"When's the last time you wrote about him?"

"Last night. I covered a story on his brutal murder of seven boy scouts. They were camping when they got hacked up. I did an interview with their scout leader. He said he was tied up and could only watch as this mad man murdered his troops. The killer told him he was kept alive to live with the experience."

"That's horrible. He was responsible for all those kids," Diane said.

Ashley pulled her car into the train station. "Well it looks like were here."

"Thank you, ladies," Charlie said, exiting the car.

"Maybe we can pick you up again," Ashley continued.

"I'm sorry, but I'll be out of town until the holiday's. Can I look you girls up when I get back?"

"You sure can," Ashley said. "We're over at the University. Either ask for Ashley Mehan, or Diane Francisco.

"Okay, I just might do that."

"Bye," Diane shouted, as they drove away.

"Do you believe those stories?" Ashley asked.

"No, but he was creepy."

"No, he wasn't."

"Yes, he was." Diane said.

"Oh, great," Ashley said, and pulled over to the side the road.

"What? What are you doing?" Diane asked nervously.

"We have a flat."

The Neighbor

It was a brisk morning on the third day of September. Summer was fading, as the wind blew debris in front of the two big houses. The two houses stood close together, side by side. One of the houses has been vacant for many years. The other was the home by a man named Edward Turner.

Edward lied in bed as the dawn light peeked through his bedroom window. The light, however, didn't bother him it was the alarm on his clock which stirred him. He reached over and turned it off. Edward pulled the blanket off his body and rose out of bed, yawned and rubbed his tired eyes.

Putting on his dark green robe, he walked into the kitchen, and started his breakfast by turning on his coffee maker, then headed to the front door to retrieve the newspaper.

The morning air was brisk as he stood on his front porch. He picked up the morning paper, which was always on his welcome mat. If it weren't, he would certainly have a complaint for his paperboy.

A deep breath filled his lungs with the cool fresh air, and then exhaled. *Retirement at its fullest.* Edward thought. *I'm 68, no wife, no kids, and I'm living my life the way I want to. Quietly.*

Edward entered his house and placed the newspaper on the kitchen table. He opened up the cabinet, grabbed a coffee mug, and poured his morning breakfast into it. He walked back over to the kitchen table where his newspaper was waiting. Life is good.

As a rule, refused to read anything except the weather and comics. He didn't want to know anything else about the world, and ignored the headline, "Murder In Small Town," and turned to see what Dagwood and Blondie were up to.

Later that day, Edward was out mowing his lawn. The mower was loud enough that he never heard the car coming down the road. After the fifth row of his lawn was completed, he shut off the engine and removed the grass-filled bag. A noise behind him pulled his attention to the black sports car that just passed him. He watched as it drove up the driveway of the abandoned house. The car stopped and waited.

That's strange. Edward thought. *Why is that car all the way out here? Especially there at the old house. Why that house has been empty for about 15 years. Could I really deal with a new neighbor?* Edward didn't know how to feel.

The door of the black sports car opened and a dark hair man got out. He wore a long black trench coat and dark sunglasses.

The man walked towards him.

"Hello, I'm Edward Turner," Edward started the conversation and held out his hand. But, Edward received no response from the man.

"Moving in, huh?"

The man stayed silent as he looked around his surroundings.

"Look, if we're going to be-"

The man cut Edward off. "Do you have a phone?"

"No! No, I don't have one. I like things quiet. But you can find one at Odie's Bar and Grill. They also have beer, for those who like to loosen up after work and such."

The man tilted his head down to look at Edward eye to eye.

"Oh!" He gave the directions nervously under the man's uncomfortable glare. Just go down this road, make your first right, then go about eight miles. It's on your left. Can't miss it."

The man turned away and went back to his black sports car. Edward just shook his head and continued his yard work.

That night Edward was sitting down in front of his TV, a local news station suddenly interrupted the show he was watching.

"Police are still on the lookout for the suspect in the murder of Mrs. Joyce Larner and her 9 year-old child Lynn Larner. Police believe it was this man, John Larner, the husband and father of the victims."

As the newswoman continued, a picture of John Larner flashed up on Edward's television screen. His tired eyes widened when the familiar face appeared in front of him. He couldn't believe it. The man on his TV screen resembled his next-door neighbor. Edward felt his heart sink and his blood pressure rise.

"Police found the two victims upstairs in the Larner home." The news anchor reported. "Police also found an axe next to their bodies. An excessive search has begun for John Larner, he is believed to be extremely dangerous."

Edward snapped off the set. *What am I going to do?* Edward wondered. *I need to call the police, but how? I have no phone. I don't even have a car. I wonder if I can make it to Odie's. That's eight miles. I can walk that. But what if he's waiting for me when I pass his house?*

All he could do was sit and wait. Wait and listen. Listen to every creak of the settling house. Every chirp from the crickets outside. Listen as the wind howled against the old, unsteady shutters. He tossed and turned in the chair. The noises grew louder. The wind blew violently, and the crickets' seem to triple in numbers.

Edward wondered if all these noise were only in his head. He felt his heart beating faster, then louder. The wind blew hard against his shutters. A loud crash made Edward leap from the chair and onto the floor. Then everything went quiet around him. He could hear nothing, but silence.

He went to the kitchen and filled a glass of water. He looked outside his kitchen window and stared at his neighbor's house. The house seemed more intimidating in the darkness, none of the lights were lit, except the attic light.

This man has murdered his family. Edward began to panic. *He's been on the news. The police are after him. He must know that I'm aware of him. He'll be after me next.* Edward glanced out the window once more and noticed the attic light had been turned off.

The pounding in Edward's heart started to move to his head, sweat poured down his face. He ran to the hallway closet and pulled out his shotgun. He had never used it before, but he felt something had to be done. Violently shaking, he grabbed the shotgun shells off the top shelf and loaded the gun. The pounding in his head turned into an excruciating hammer hitting against his brain. He raced to the front door, the wind stirred up the leaves all around him, as he ran out onto his porch.

Red and blue lights flashed all around him. Police cars engulfed his neighbor's driveway. Relief filled Edward's body and his heartbeat slowed down. He felt safe once again and lowered the shotgun and then walked back into the house. It was all over.

The next morning, Edward was outside doing some yard work. He picked up the dead branches and sticks off his lawn from the strong gust of wind last night.

He heard a car coming down the road. He didn't think much of it at first, but the car sounded as if it were slowing down. Edward turned and looked. There in the driveway was the black sports car and his neighbor stepped out.

Edward was in shock, as he stared at the familiar man exiting the car.

"Good morning," the man said, walking inside the house and closing the door.

Edward could not believe his eyes. He dropped the sticks to the ground, and the noises in his head started to pound once again. He ran up his front porch and back inside, hastily, looking around, he saw what he wanted. He picked up his shotgun that he left lying next to the couch. Edward went back out, and ran to his neighbor's house

He quietly entered, as his breath became hard and heavy. Edward's head started to beat to the sounds of cannon fire. He walked into the first room. It was empty. No furniture, no carpet, the only thing he saw were a few boxes stacked up against the wall.

He saw a door to his left, and slowly opened it. There he found stairs that climbed up to the attic. Edward was about to go up until he heard a noise coming from the room behind him, backing out of the attic's doorway, he came to a sliding wooden door, carefully and slowly he slid the door away from him.

His neighbor stood with his back towards Edward. Sweat dripped off his face, as he raised the shotgun and aimed it at the man. His hands were shaking, the pounding in his head grew louder, as he held the shotgun tighter and inched his finger toward the trigger.

The man turned around from making his jelly sandwich and saw Edward standing in front of him. Another loud sound echoed through the kitchen. But it was not from Edward's head, but from his shotgun. He watched the man being knocked back from the blast, falling with a thud onto the floor.

Edward thought it was all over once again, but the pounding in his head still continued. He turned around and looked to the attic door.

"I know you're still here somewhere," he shouted, believing that the noise was coming from somewhere in the house, and not from his head. "I can still hear you!"

Up the attic stairs he ran, and when he reached the top, he saw a large wooden create. He walked slowly over to it and opened the lid. The empty crate was layered with dry bloodstains.

"My head. Make it stop!" He was almost in tears from the pain. Edward started to run back down the steps, but lost his balance. He tumbled and crashed hard onto the floor.

Edward stayed there as calmly as he could, but the noises in his head became louder and louder. He looked down on the floor and saw his shotgun lying beside him. Edward picked it up and raised it to his head. The last sound that Edward would ever hear echoed through the house. And, finally, there was silence.

At Odie's Bar and Grill, the bartender raised the volume on the TV set that hung above the bar. The anchorwoman began to speak.

"In later news, John Larner was turned in yesterday to authorities by his own twin brother, Joseph Larner. John agreed to meet Joseph at his new house. He had asked John to turn himself in. When refused, a scuffle broke out between the two. John became wounded during the dispute. Joseph Larner decided to keep John in a large moving crate until police could arrive. This is Carol Writhers for the six o'clock news."

A Warm Place to Stay

Neal thought about the mistakes he had made in his past. He looked down at his tattered clothes, his old torn coat, and his empty whiskey bottle. He regretted them all. Neal sat there in the small park and looked up into the sky as the snow fell down over his unshaved face, he asked God why life had made him a bum. Was there no hope for him? Was this his end?

The morning crowd started to walk by him, but he would never look up at them. He felt to ashamed for the state he was in. Neal also felt if he did look up at them, he would see what he was missing, happiness. Usually no one spoke to him, they just moved about their lives. However, yesterday was different. A clean-cut businessman approached him.

"Would you like a free meal and a warm place to stay?" Neal thought about the question the man had asked.

But he never answered the man, he simply looked back down and waited for him to leave.

He wondered why a stranger would want to help a poor bum like himself. Could it be that there was some kindness left in the world? With this question burning in his mind, he prepared for a very frigid night and finally fell asleep.

Neal awoke and stumbled to his feet. He felt dizzy from lack of nourishment. Someone clutched his arm, and helped him to balance his legs. He looked over and saw the same man from the other day. The man was shaven and had nicely groomed hair. He wore an expensive looking overcoat and a professional suit underneath.

"Are you Okay?" The man asked.

Neal could only nod back.

"Would you like a free meal and a warm place to stay?"

Neal stared into the man's eyes. He wondered if he should go or not. It has been many days since he had eaten last, but he did not say a word and watched as the businessman walked away. Neal wanted to say yes, it was on the tip of his tongue. But no words followed. As the day wore on, the man didn't come back and Neal felt he had lost his chance.

Neal stumbled over to the closest park bench and stretched out across the uncomfortable cold metal. He pulled his coat as tightly as he could around himself, but his body started to shake and his lips quivered from the bitter cold.

"Are you sure you are okay?" A voice said.

Neal looked up and couldn't believe his eyes. The businessman came back. Maybe there was hope. This time he wouldn't hesitate.

"Would you like a free meal and a warm place to stay?" The man asked again.

Neal gleamed a smile with his rotten black teeth. "Yes." He said hoarsely.

"Follow me."

"Who are you?" Neal felt that he should ask. "Are you an angel?"

"No," the man chuckled. "You can call me James."

Neal followed James out from the park and into the busy city. He watched the busses and cars as they drove by. He saw people rushing by him. Some people walk hand in hand or pushing a baby stroller, this made him realize what was incomplete in his life, marriage, and having a family. Earning a living, and buying a home. He knew that this was what he wanted, and maybe he would be able to have it.

Neal decided that once he got cleaned up at James' home, he was going to find a job and be somebody important. Someone like James, he felt James had all this. He imaged James living in a nice big house with a wrap around porch and a white picket fence, with a beautiful and talented wife, two kids who were wonderful and going to private school. To have a life like he imagined James to have, this would be his goal.

He followed James into an unclean building, and up three flights of litter filled stairs. He watched James stopped in front of a door and slowly opened it. James advised Neal to walked into the room first.

The room was very small and all the windows were either cracked or missing. Most of the wall-paper was ripped and hanging off. In the middle of the bare wooden floor was a small and dirty cot.

Certainly this was a mistake! James the businessman did not live here. This was not what he expected at all.

Neal turned around, and saw James holding an axe. He had no time to move, as he watched James lift the axe over his head. The blade of the axe came down forcefully and sliced into Neal's flesh

James left the room with Neal's body lying across the floor. He went down the three flights of stairs, and out of the building to find a payphone and dial 911.

When the police had arrived, James showed them the body in his room. He proudly admitted killing the bum. He was placed under arrest and was brought to the holding block.

The police locked him into a small cell until they could further question him. James looked over to his cellmate.

"What are you in for?" James asked the cell-mate.

"I didn't do a thing." The man answered.

"What about you, what are you in for?"

James snickered to himself, then said. "Me, I'm here for a free meal and a warm place to stay."

I am Not A Mad Man

Hello, my name is Phillip, and I'm a serial killer. That was the thought that ran through my head last night.

The morning sun shined into my room and woke me without warning. I tried to close my eyes tighter, but was unsuccessful. I had to face the fact that it was time to wake up. I knew that the floor would be cold before my feet landed on the hardwood. I searched for my old pair of socks. The rest of my clothes I didn't have to worry about. I'd slept in them.

Once dressed, I stumbled out of the room into a hallway crowded with empty beer bottles and crumbled old newspapers. This reminded me of where I was.

Living in this downtown motel was not something to invite mother to. Sometimes I didn't know which was worse, having no lock on my rented door or walking down to the end of the hall to use an unlit bathroom.

I stepped out onto what is known as the "lifeless" part of the city, no one but the homeless walked these streets. Sometimes, I would feel like one of them. Not knowing where I was going in life, and not too sure where life would take me. I did my best to try not to look like one of them. But when I'm talking to the city folks, it's hard to explain the dried-up blood stains on my white shirt. Just call it being in the wrong place at the wrong time. I'm still not certain whose blood it was. Was it the pimp's or the prostitute's? I guess it doesn't really matter now.

The wind blew through my ripped overcoat. The tall buildings would hide the morning sun until the afternoon. I hated winter. The hardest part on a winter's day was looking for food. Wait, make that the second hardest. The hardest was carrying around this axe without anyone seeing it. When people see you trying to hide an axe under your coat, they usually don't like to stick around. Most of them would run away screaming, as if I was carrying their decapitated head around.

Don't get me wrong. I wasn't always like this. I had a wife named Susan, two kids, and a great job. Then, one day, I came home early to find my kids playing in the backyard, while my best friend is in bed with my wife.

Sometimes I think life can't get any worse. Then I find out that my wife gets the house. The house I paid for, the deck that I built, that nice garden I planted, and the pool. And don't forget the swing set for the kids. That's nice. So even though she gets all that, she's still sleeping with my best friend. The kids get a new uncle named Ralph, and lucky me, I get to pay alimony and child support.

So I quit my job, because I'm sick of the gossip about my wife being murdered. My boss demotes me, says he feels he cannot trust me anymore, and thinks it's the best thing for the company. But soon enough everyone finds out that those murders are reality. Susan's body *was* hacked up into tiny pieces.

So I make sure that I move to a place where I'll never be found. My secret place, if you will. But when the money fades away, you find yourself stealing and going through garbage cans.

Suddenly the crime of stealing from others soon gets out of control, and then I start to wonder if my victims will tell the police. Now I have to make sure that they can't tell a soul. I would have preferred a knife, but all I could find was this rusted axe in a dumpster behind a Wal-Mart.

I do have to say, when I first took a person's life, all I could think was that I would never do it again. First of all, it's not an easy task, especially when going through their wallet and see pictures of their family. That's always a tough one. But throughout the weeks, I have to say it has gotten easier, almost enjoyable.

Did you know that the average adult has about five liters of blood in their body. It's funny seeing my victims fight with all their energy, trying so hard to keep every ounce of it. With only three hacks from my axe, I can see their body convulsing from the loss of blood.

Once their supply of oxygen is cut off, the brain cannot function normally. They become paralyzed, and then their sensory perception starts to go. Brain damage sets in. Finally death.

Now, I'm not saying I hate human life, or that our world has fallen into greed for money. People will always fight for the dollar sign. They don't realize, like I do, that we were not put on this earth to become rich, or to become beggars. We are here to survive, and survive by any means possible.

With that always in my mind, I don't feel like a crazed lunatic when I take someone's life.

Most people never think that an axe-murdering psychopath would kill them. It never even crosses their mind. Statistics say people are more likely to die by suicide then murder. Did you know more than 30,000 Americans commit suicide each year? People die every day and in so many horrible ways. Why should my way be any different?

I know it's against the law to kill a human being, but what about nature's law? If you look at the animal world, they kill every day. Not only do they kill other species, but also their own. It's all about survival.

There are other questions I ask myself. Like, am I really that different? If they found me today, would they call me insane for what I've done? Would they think I'm dangerous, or that I have demons inside of me? Would they be made to believe that I see visions of dragons in my sleep? Would they imprison me within four mental walls, or would they think that I just had a crude hatred towards human life? Is this just a phase?

If they did catch me, I know society would call me names. I say let them call me an intruder, killer, or a homicidal maniac. Let them call me which ever they like. Doctors and therapists would say that I was deranged, that I was an outcast, and didn't follow the rules of society. They might say that my human mind is complex, and filled with anger.

I would disagree. However, I am an outcast of the system. A system of laws and orders that I felt were unjust. When I stopped following the system, I was abused, abandoned, and left for dead. But I never hung my head in shame. Instead I got even. Even with my wife, with my boss, and with society.

It didn't take any voices in my head, nor a doll with needles. I used my axe and hacked my victims like pieces of meat.

Many people don't realize that our world may not live forever. One night the sunrise might never come, the sky will turn black. Evil could one day rule our world, or maybe it has already begun.